THE DOOM FROM PLANET 4

THE DOOM FROM PLANET 4

by Jack Williamson

A ray of fire, green, mysterious, stabs through the night to Dan on his ship. It leads him to an island of unearthly peril.

"S O S. S O S. S O S." Three short, three long, three short, the flashes winked from the dark headland. Dan McNally, master and owner of the small and ancient trading schooner, *Virginia*, caught the feeble flickering light from the island as he strode across the fore-deck. He stopped, stared at the looming black line of land beneath the tropical stars. Again light flashed from a point of rock far above the dim white line of phosphorescent surf, spelling out the signal of distress.

*

"Somebody bane callin' with a flashlight, It'ank," the big Swede, Larsen, rumbled from the wheel.

Dan thought suddenly of a reply. He rushed into the charthouse, to return in a moment with a lighted lantern and a copy of the *Nautical Almanac* which would serve to hide the flame between flashes. He flashed an answer.

Again the pale light flickered from the dark mass of land, spelling words out rather slowly, as if the sender were uncertain in his knowledge of Morse. Surprised as Dan had been by the signal from an island marked on the charts as uninhabited, he was astonished at the message that now came to him.

"You are in terrible danger," he read in the flashes. "Dreadful thing here. Hurry away. Radio for warships. I am—"

The winking light suddenly went out. Dan strained his eyes to watch the point where it had been, and a few seconds later he saw a curious thing. A darting, stabbing lance of green fire flashed out across the barren, rocky cliff, lighting it fleetingly with pale green radiance. It leapt out and was gone in an instant, leaving the shoulder of the island dark as before.

Dan watched for long minutes, but he saw nothing more brilliant than the pale gleam of phosphorescence where the waves dashed against the sheer granite wall of the island.

"What you t'ank?" Larsen broke in upon him.

*

Dan started, then answered slowly. "I don't know. First I thought there must be a lunatic at large. But that green light! I didn't like it."

5

THE DOOM FROM PLANET 4

He stared again at the looming mass of the island. Davis Island is one of the innumerable tiny islets that dot the South Pacific; merely the summit of a dead volcano, projecting above the sea. Nominally claimed by Great Britain, it is marked on the charts as uninhabited.

"Radio for warships, eh?" he muttered. A wireless transmitter was one of many modern innovations that the *Virginia* did not boast. She had been gathering copra and shell among the islands long before such things came into common use, though Dan had invested his modest savings in her only a year before.

"What would anyone want with warships on Davis Island?" The name roused a vague memory. "Davis Island?" he repeated, staring in concentration at the black sea. "Of course!" It came to him suddenly. A newspaper article that he had read five years before, at about the time he had abandoned college in the middle of his junior year, to follow the call of adventure.

The account had dealt with an eclipse of the sun, visible only from certain points on the Pacific. One Dr. Hunter, under the auspices of a Western university, had sailed with his instruments and assistants to Davis Island, to study the solar corona during the few precious moments when the shadow covered the sun, and to observe the displacement of certain stars as a test of Einstein's theory of relativity.

The reporter had interviewed the party at San Francisco, on the eve of sailing. There had been photographs of the chartered vessel, of Dr. Hunter and his instruments, and of his daughter, Helen, who acted as his secretary. She looked not at all like a scientist, Dan recalled. In fact, her face had seemed rather pretty, even in the blurred newspaper half-tone.

But the memory cast no light upon the present puzzle. In the rambling years that had led him to this spot upon the old *Virginia*, he had lost touch with the science that had interested him during his college days. He had heard nothing of the results of the Hunter expedition. But this island had been its destination.

*

He turned decisively to the man at the wheel. "Larsen, we'll stand well offshore till daylight," he said. "Then, unless we see something unusual, we can sail in and land a boat to—"

The sentence was never finished. Through the corner of his eye, Dan saw a ray of green light darting toward them from the island. A line of green fire seemed to reach out and strike him a physical blow. Green flame flared around him; and somehow he was hurled from the bridge, clear of the rail and into the sea.

His impression of the incident was very confused. He seemed to have struck the water with such force that his breath was knocked out. He struggled back to the surface, strangling, and coughing the bitter brine from his lungs. It was several minutes before he was comfortably treading water, and able to see what had happened.

The old schooner was then a hundred yards away, careening crazily, and drifting aimlessly before the light breeze. The strange green fire had vanished. Parts of the ship apparently had been carried away or disintegrated by the ray or the force of which it was a visible effect. The mainmast was down, and was hanging over the side in a tangle of rigging.

Bright yellow flames were dancing at a dozen points about the wreckage on the listing deck. A grotesque broken thing, queerly illuminated by the growing fires, was hanging over the wheel—the body of Larsen. No living thing was visible; and Dan, after a second look at the wreck of the bow, knew that he must be the sole survivor of the catastrophe.

"Too bad about the boys," he muttered through teeth that chattered, for the cold water had already chilled him. "And poor old Larsen."

He thought again of the warning flashed from the shore. "Guess there must be something hellish afoot after all," he muttered again. "The flicker of green that stopped the signals, and the green fire that got us—what can they mean?" He looked toward the looming black shadow of the island, and began divesting himself of his clinging, sodden garments. "I don't wonder somebody wanted battleships. But even a battleship, if that green ray hit it—"

He drew a deep breath and ducked his head while he unlaced his shoes and kicked out of them. Then, with a final look at the burning wreck of the *Virginia*, he tore off the last bit of his underclothing and swam for the shore in an easy crawl.

*

The rocky ramparts of Davis Island were three or four miles away. But there was no wind; the black sea was calm save for a long, hardly perceptible swell. A strong swimmer and in superb condition, Dan felt no anxiety about being able to make the distance. There was danger, however, that a shark would run across him, or that he could not find a landing place upon the rocky shore.

Four bells had rung when he had seen the first flash; it had been just ten o'clock. And it was some four hours later that Dan touched bottom and waded wearily up a bit of smooth hard beach, through palely glittering phosphorescent foam.

He rubbed the brine from his tired limbs, and sat down for a time, in a spot where a fallen boulder sheltered his naked body from the cool morning wind. In a few moments he rose, flexed his muscles and peered through the starlit darkness for a way up the cliff behind the beach. He found it impossible to distinguish anything.

"Got to keep moving, or find some clothes," he muttered. "And I may stumble onto what made the green light. Darn lucky I've been so far, anyhow. Larsen and the others—but I shan't think of them. Wonder who was flashing the signals from the island. And did the green fire get him?"

He turned to look out over the black plain of the sea. Far out, the *Virginia* lay low in the water, a pillar of yellow flame rising from her hull. As he watched, the flame flickered and vanished: the old schooner, he supposed, had sunk. Then he noticed a pale glow come into being among the stars on the eastern horizon.

"Hello," he muttered again. "So we're going to have a moon? In the last quarter, but still it ought to light me up from this beach."

A moment later the horns of the crescent had come above the black rim of the sea. Dan waited, swinging his arms and tramping up and down on the sand, until the silvery moon had cleared the horizon and illuminated the rugged face of the cliff with pale white radiance.

He chose a path to the top of the cliff and clambered up, emerging in a jungle-like thicket of brush. Picking his way with the greatest caution, yet scratching his naked skin most painfully, he made his way for a few yards through the brush to a point of vantage from which he could look about.

He was, he perceived, in a narrow valley or ravine, with rugged black walls rising sheer on either side. The silvery light of the crescent moon fell upon the rank jungle that covered the narrow floor of the canyon, which rose and dwindled as it penetrated inland.

*

Gazing up the canyon, Dan gasped in amazement at what he saw.

Mars, the red planet, hung bright and motionless, low in the western sky, gleaming with deep bloody radiance. Directly beneath it, bathed in the white light of the moon, was a bare, rocky peak that seemed the highest point of the island. And upon that highest pinnacle, that chanced to be just below the ruddy star, was an astounding machine.

Three slender towers, of a white metal that gleamed in the moonlight with the silvery luster of aluminum, rose from the rocky peak. They supported, in a horizontal position, an enormous metal ring. It must be, Dan reckoned swiftly, at least a hundred feet in diameter, and held a hundred feet above the summit of the mountain.

The huge ring gleamed with a strange purple radiance. A shimmering mist of red-violet light surrounded it. An unknown force seemed to throb within the mighty ring, drawing the mantle of purple haze about it.

And suspended inside the ring and below it was a long, slender needle of dazzling white light. To Dan, from where he stood in the canyon, it seemed a fine, sharp line, though he knew it must be some kind of pointer, luminous with the strange force pulsing through it.

9

THE DOOM FROM PLANET 4

The strange needle wavered a little, with quick, uncertain motions. The brilliance of its light varied oddly; it seemed to throb with a queer, irregular rhythm.

And the gleaming needle pointed straight at the planet Mars!

Dan stood a long time, watching the purple ring upon the silver towers, with the shining white needle hanging below it. He stared at Mars, glowing like a red and sinister eye above the incredible mechanism.

His mind was in a wild storm of wonder shot with fear. What was the meaning of the gleaming ring and needle? What connection did this great device have with the signal of distress from the cliff, and the green fire that had destroyed the *Virginia*? And why did the glowing needle point at Mars?

*

He did not know when he first began to hear the sound. For a time it was merely part of the strange mystery of the island, only another element in the atmosphere of fear and wonder that surrounded him. Then it rose a little, and he became suddenly sharply conscious of it as an additional menace. The sound was not loud, but deep and vibrant. A whir or hum, like that of a powerful, muffled motor, but deeper than the sound of any motor man has ever made. It came down the gorge, from the direction of the machine on the mountain.

That deep, throbbing noise frightened Dan as none of his previous experiences had done. Shivering from fear as much as from cold, he crouched down beside a huge boulder in the edge of the tangle of brush that covered the bottom of the ravine. His heart pounded wildly. He was in the clutches of an unreasoning fear that some terrible Thing had seen him, and was about to seek him out. For a moment he had to use all his will to keep himself from panic flight through the brush. The unknown is always terrible, and he had invaded the domain of a force he could not understand.

In a moment, however, he recovered himself. He would be as safe there in the jungle, he thought, as anywhere on the island. He thought of starting a fire, then realized that he had no matches, and that he would not dare to make a light if he were able. He pulled a few handfuls of dry grass to make a sort of bed, upon which he huddled up, thanking his lucky stars that the island was in semi-tropical latitudes.

His mind returned again to the riddles that confronted him: the green flash and the strange mechanism on the peak. He recalled fantastic stories he had read, of hermit scientists conducting amazing experiments in isolated parts of the world. Presently he decided that something of the kind must be on foot here.

"The green flash is a sort of a death ray," he summed up, aloud. "And they shoot it from that bright needle. No wonder they don't want to be bothered! Somebody may be fixing to upset civilization!

"But it's queer that the needle points at Mars...."

Of this last fact, which might have been a clue to the most reasonable solution of the mystery, if a rather astounding one, he was able to make nothing. In fact, huddled up on his pile of grass in some degree of comfort, he presently went to sleep, still pondering in vain upon this last clue.

*

He was awakened by a soft, insistent purring sound, rather like that of a small electric motor run without load at very high speed. Recollection of the night's events came abruptly to him, and he sprang to his feet in alarm, finding his muscles sore and stiff from his cramped position.

From one side Dan heard the rumble of thunder, and, glancing up, saw that the sky above the sea was overcast with a rolling mass of dark, menacing clouds. There was a strange portentous blackness about these storm clouds that filled him with a nameless fear.

Suddenly he was struck with the thought that it was not thunder that had wakened him. The noise he had heard had not the rumbling or booming quality of thunder. As he stood there he again became conscious of the low, whirring sound, behind him. He whirled around to face it. The shock of what he saw left him momentarily dizzy and trembling—though undoubtedly his surroundings had much to do with its effect upon him.

The sound came from a glistening metal machine which stood half-hidden in the brush a dozen yards away *looking at him!*

THE DOOM FROM PLANET 4

The thing was made of a lustrous, silvery metal, which Dan afterwards supposed to be aluminum, or some alloy of that metal. Its gleaming case was shaped more like a coffin, or an Egyptian mummy-case, than any other object with which he was familiar, though rather larger than either.

That is, it was an oblong metal box, tapering toward the ends, with the greatest width forward of the middle. Twin tubes projected from the end of it, lenses in them glistening like eyes. Just below them sprang out steely, glistening tentacles several feet long, writhing and twitching as if they were alive. The tangle of green brush hid the thing's legs, so that Dan could not see them.

*

Suddenly it sprang toward him, rising ten feet high and covering half the distance between them. It alighted easily upon the two long, jointed metal limbs upon which it had leapt, and continued to keep the lens-tubes turned toward Dan, so he knew that the grotesque metal thing was *watching him.*

The limbs, he observed, were similar to the hind legs of a grasshopper, both in shape and position. And evidently the thing leapt upon them in about the same way. Then he noticed another curious thing about it.

Three little bars of metal projected above the thickest part of its case, on the upper side. Their ends were joined by a little ring, three inches across. The tiny metal ring glowed with purple luminosity. A purple haze seemed to cling about it, as to the huge ring Dan had seen on the towers above the peak. And suspended inside this ring was a tiny metal needle, shimmering with pulsating white fire.

On the back of this metal monster was a miniature replica of the strange mechanism upon the pinnacle. The little needle pointed up the canyon. A glance that way showed Dan that it pointed at the great device upon the mountain, which looked even more brilliant on this gloomy morning than in the uncertain radiance of the moon. The colossal ring was shrouded in a splendid mantle of purple flame; and the long, slender needle, which seemed to have swung on down to follow Mars below the horizon, still throbbed with scintillating white fire.

12

For several minutes the two stood there, studying each other. A naked man, tense and bewildered in the presence of mysterious forces—and a grotesque machine, cased in gleaming white metal, whose parts seemed to duplicate most of the functions of a living creature.

Then one of the writhing tentacles that shot from the "head" of the machine reached back under the metal case, and reappeared grasping what appeared to be a flat disk of emerald, two inches across and half an inch thick.

This green disk it held up, with a flat side toward Dan. There was no sound, but a flash of green light came from it, cutting a wide swath into the jungle, and littering its path with smoking and flaming debris.

*

But Dan, expecting something of the kind, had flung himself sidewise into the shelter of the boulder beside which he had slept. Behind it, he gathered his feet under him, picked up a rock of convenient size for throwing, and waited, ready and alert.

He heard the soft humming sound on the other side of the boulder. A glittering object flashed above him. Crashing through the brush the metal monster came to earth on the same side of the boulder with him.

But the metal thing had not turned in its flight: consequently its rear end was toward Dan. As it began cumberously to turn about, he hurled his rock with an accuracy that came of a boyhood on the farm. Instinct had made him try for the little ring and needle on the back of the monster, apparently its most vulnerable part.

Whether by luck or skill, the rock struck the gleaming ring, crushing it against the needle—and instant paralysis overtook the metal thing. Its tentacles and limbs became fixed and rigid, and it toppled over in the brush.

Dan walked over to it, and examined it briefly. The green disk had fallen on the ground, and he picked it up. It was made of emerald crystal, it had a little knob of glistening metal set in one side. Rather afraid of it, Dan forebore to twist the knob. But he still clutched it in his hand a few moments later, when, partly for fear that others of its kind would come to succor the

13

fallen monster, and partly to secure shelter from the threatening rain, he retired into the shadows of the tangled jungle.

He spent perhaps half an hour in creeping back to what he supposed a place of comparative safety. For some time he lay there in the cool gloom, brushing occasional insects off his bare skin, wishing by turns that he had a cup of coffee and a good beefsteak, and that he could puzzle out a logical solution of all the astounding things he had met in the island. After the encounter with the metal monster, he felt his theory of the hermit scientists a bit inadequate.

*

Presently his attention was attracted by the unmistakable mew of a kitten. Then he heard the padding sound of cautious human footsteps, and a clear feminine voice calling "Kitty, kitty," in low tones. The steps and the voice seemed coming toward him; since there was no sound of crackling brush, he supposed there was a trail which he had not found.

"Hello," he ventured, when the voice seemed only a few yards away through the green tangle.

At the same instant a gray kitten appeared out of the underbrush, and frisked trustfully across to him. He put out a hand, caressed it, picked it up. In a moment the feminine voice replied, "Hello yourself. Who are you?"

A crackling sound came from the brush, as if the speaker were starting toward him. Dan, abruptly conscious of his lack of attire, said quickly, "Wait a minute! I haven't anything on, you see. I'm Dan McNally. I owned the schooner that something happened to off the island last night."

A delicious, trilling laugh greeted the panic of his first words. Then the clear, sweet voice, serious again, replied, "So you swam ashore from the boat I signaled?"

"Yes."

"Gee, but I'm glad to find you! And you say you haven't any clothes? I wonder what...." The voice paused reflectively, then resumed, "Here's a sheet that I got to signal with in the daytime, if I had a chance. You might wrap it around you until we find something better."

The low, liquid laugh rang out again; again there was a rustling in the brush, and presently an arm appeared, holding a rolled-up sheet.

"All right," he called. "Throw it this way."

*

In a moment, with the sheet draped around him like a Roman toga, and the kitten on his arm, he advanced to meet the owner of the beautiful voice.

At the trail he met a trim, active-looking young woman, clad in out-of-door attire and with a canvas knapsack on her back. Bareheaded, she wore her brown hair closely shingled. Her face, Dan recognized from the photograph he had seen five years before, though it was more lovely than the splotched newspaper picture had hinted. Her brown eyes were filled with laughter at his predicament and his present unusual garb.

He bowed with mock gravity and said, "How do you do, Miss Helen Hunter?"

Brown eyes widened in surprise. "You know me?" she asked.

"Not half so well as I hope to," he grinned.

Then, handing her the kitten, he spoke seriously. "What about this island? The green flashes? The big machine on the mountain? The metal thing that jumps about like a grasshopper? What's it all about? You know anything about it?"

"Yes, I know a good deal about it," she told him soberly. "It's rather a terrible story. And one you may not believe—no, you've seen them! But the kitten is hungry, and you must be, too, if you swam ashore."

"Well, yes, I am." Dan admitted.

The storm clouds were drifting out to sea; the sun was beginning to assert itself, and it now lighted up the scene with a cheerful brightness. She slung off her pack and sat down cross-legged at the side of the trail. Dan sat down opposite her as she opened the knapsack and produced a can of condensed milk, one of sardines, a can-opener, and half a loaf of bread.

15

"I had to select my supplies rather at random," she said, "and you'll have to make the best of them."

She started to open the sardines. "You'd better give it to me," Dan advised. "You might cut your hand."

"You think so?" she asked, deftly lifting the lid, fishing out a fish for the kitten, and presenting the can to Dan. Then with capable hands she broke off a large chunk of bread, which she handed him.

"Go ahead and finish this up," she said. "I've already had breakfast." She punched two holes in the end of the milk can, and poured some of the thick yellow fluid into the palm of her left hand, from which she let the kitten lap it.

"And now for the mystery of the island," Dan demanded, forgetting bread and sardines in his eagerness.

*

The girl turned her face to him. "I'm Helen Hunter, as you seem to know," she began. "I came here with my father five years ago to observe an eclipse of the sun. When it was all over, and the ship called to take us off, he decided to send the results of our observations by one of the other men. He wanted to stay here to carry on another experiment—the one that led to that machine on the hill. Part of the other men were willing to stay. The yacht left us here, and has been back from San Francisco every six months since, with mail and supplies."

"And what was the experiment?" Dan demanded eagerly.

"Have you ever looked at Mars through a good telescope?" she countered. "Then you must have seen the canals—straight dark lines running from the white polar caps to the equatorial zone. All scientists did not agree as to what they were, but nobody could suggest a natural origin for them.

"My father was one of those who thought that the canals were fertile, cultivated strips, irrigated with water brought down from the melting ice-caps. Irrigation systems meant intelligent life upon the planet, and his experiment was an attempt to communicate with that intelligence."

"And he succeeded?" Dan was astounded.

16

"Yes. The means was simple enough: other men had suggested it years before, in fact. Any fairly bright light on Mars—such as the beam of a searchlight directed toward earth—would be visible in a good telescope, when the planet is favorably situated: it follows that such a light on earth should be visible to an observer with a similar instrument on Mars.

"It was possible, of course, but unlikely, that Mars would have intelligent inhabitants still ignorant of the telescope. It was also possible that their senses would be different from ours—that, if they saw at all, it would be with a different part of the spectrum. Father took the chance. And he succeeded.

"The call was simple: merely three flashes of light, repeated again and again. We used a portable searchlight, mounted on a motor-truck, such as is used in the army. The three flashes meant that we were on the third planet of the solar system. The answering call, from the fourth planet, should be four flashes, of course.

"For three nights we kept signaling. One of the men watched the motor-generator, and I operated the searchlight, swinging it on Mars and off again, to make the flashes. Dad kept his eye screwed to the telescope. Nothing happened and he got discouraged. I persuaded him to keep on for another night, in case they hadn't seen us at first; or needed more time to get their searchlight ready.

"And on the fourth night poor Dad came out of the observatory, shouting that he had seen four flashes."

*

Dan gasped, speechless with astonishment. "Then that machine, with the needle pointing at Mars, and the green flashes, and the thing that jumped at me—"

Helen waved a white hand for silence. "Just keep cool a minute! I'm coming to them.

"The four flashes just began it. In a few days Dad and the Martians were communicating by a sort of television process. He would mark off a sheet of paper into squares, blacken some of the squares to make a picture or design, then have me send a flash for each black square, and miss an interval for each

17

white one, taking them in regular order. The Martians seemed to catch on pretty soon; in a few days Dad was receiving pictures of the same sort.

"Rather a slow way of communication, perhaps. But it worked better than one might think at first. In a month Dad had received instructions for building a small machine like that big one on the hill. It is something like radio—at least it operates with vibrations in the ether—but it's as much ahead of our radio as an airplane is in advance of a fire-balloon. I understand a good bit about it, but I won't try to explain it now.

"And in the next three years Dad learned no end of things from the people on Mars. One queer thing about it was, that they never let us see them on the television apparatus, no matter how many of their scientific secrets they gave us. Dad and I exhibited ourselves, but I don't know yet what the Martians look like—though I have made a guess.

"By the end of the third year they had showed Dad how to make one of those metal things—"

"Like that one that jumped at me?" Dan broke in with a shudder.

"Yes. They seem almost alive; but they are machines, like our robots, and controlled by the radio apparatus. The eyes use photo-electric cells, and relay what is before them to the Master Intelligence." The girl spoke these last words in a low tone, shrinking involuntarily. She paused a moment, then shrugged and continued.

"The first machine did not obey my father. It was controlled by signals that came from Mars, over the big station on the hill. And it went to work, making more apparatus, building more machines, enlarging the receiving station. It worked in obedience to the Master Intelligence on Mars!

"That was a year ago. The last time the yacht called, my father and the other men still hoped to control the machines. They let her go back without us. The machines tolerated us a while; paid no attention to us; they were busy working mines and building huge, strange things that must be flying machines; the plateau on the other side of the peak is crowded with them.

"For the machines are preparing to leave the island! They are going to conquer the world for the Master Intelligence on Mars!

"Months ago my father discovered this, and realized that he had loosed doom upon the earth. He and the three other men planned to destroy that big station on the peak. All the signals to the machines are relayed through that, from Mars. The machines seemed to pay no heed as they made their preparations.

"Then one night, about three weeks ago, they tried to dynamite the station." The girl's shoulder trembled; she paused to brush a tear from her eye, then went on hastily, in a voice grown husky with emotion. Dan felt an odd desire to take her slight form in his arms and comfort her in her grief.

"The machines had seemed heedless, but they were ready. They had those disks that throw the green fire: we had not seen them before. And—well, all four of them were killed."

Dan handed her the disk of green crystal he had taken from the thing that had attacked him. She examined it silently, then went on.

"Dad had left me in bed, but I heard an explosion. I think the bombs went off when the green fire struck them. I knew what had happened, and got out of the house just before the machines arrived. They wrecked the place with their green flashes.

"And for the last three weeks I've been hiding in the jungle, or watching for ships. Three times I've raided the ruins of the house for something to eat: fortunately it didn't burn, like your ship. And that's all, I suppose—except I'm awfully glad that you got ashore."

"Thanks," Dan said, earnestly. "And what are we going to do now?"

*

"I don't know," Helen answered in a troubled tone. "I'm afraid. Afraid for all humanity. On the television, I've seen enough of Mars to be sure that it is a world of machines, controlled by one Master Intelligence. And even that may be a machine. We make machines that compute the tides and carry out other computations that are almost beyond the power of the human mind: why couldn't a machine think?

"The Master Intelligence of Mars plans to add the Earth to his domain. Unless we can do something to stop it, in a few years the world will be overrun with gigantic robot-machines, controlled by force from across the gulf of space. Humanity cannot resist them. Imagine a battleship pitted against that green annihilating ray, and all the other science of an elder planet!

"Life is to be blotted out! The Master Intelligence of Mars will rule two worlds of mechanical monsters!"

Dan sat in a dazed vision of horror to come, until Helen straightened up as if shaking off a mantle of fear, and smiled heroically, if a bit wanly.

"Now you must eat your bread and sardines, to give you strength to fight for humanity!" she cried, with a laugh that she strived, not too successfully, to make cheerful and gay.

Obediently, he began to eat, finding an excellent appetite....

It was several minutes later that he fancied he heard a whirring and crackling in the brush behind them. He sprang to his feet in alarm.

"It can't be far back to where I left the machine," he cried. "Do you suppose there's danger that—"

The mechanical ears of the metal things may have picked up the sound of his voice: but in any event, green flame flashed about them on the instant. Feeling a sudden protective impulse, Dan started toward Helen. That was his last recollection, before what seemed a terrific concussion swept him into the abyss of unconsciousness....

*

His first thought, when he awakened, was of the girl. But he was alone in the silence of the canyon. He sat up, realizing that many hours had passed, for the air was growing cool again, and the sun was low behind the peak at the head of the ravine. The huge, mysterious machine of the purple ring and the vibrating white needle were blazing splendidly.

He took more detailed stock of his immediate surroundings. The tangle of brush that had sheltered them had been cut away by the green annihilating ray. Charred stumps remained to show where it had fired bushes beyond the trail. His own shoulder was blistered, a hole was burned in the sheet wound about him, and the hair was singed from the back of his head.

Suddenly trembling with horror, he looked about for anything to show that Helen had perished by the ray. Discovering nothing, he breathed a sigh of relief.

"She must be still alive, anyhow," he muttered. "And I've had another lucky break! The ray was too high to get me. They must have left me for dead."

Presently he became conscious of torturing thirst. He retired through the brush, along the rocky wall of the canyon. By sunset he came upon a little natural basin in a rock, half full of rain water. It was none too clean, but he drank his fill of it, and felt relief.

Looking up the canyon, he could see the great mechanism on the peak, gleaming in the dusk. Intensely-glowing purple mist clung about the great metal ring, and the slender, delicate needle swung below it, still vibrating, still throbbing with brilliant, white radiance. It pointed at the red eye of Mars, which had just winked into view.

Dan stared at it a long time.

"It all sounds crazy," he muttered, "but it isn't! The Master Intelligence of Mars, she said, is controlling the mechanical things through that! The doom of the Earth is coming through that white needle! If only I could smash it, somehow!"

He looked down at the white folds of the sheet that draped him, and clenched his hands impotently. "No gun! Not even a pocket-knife. Nothing but my bare hands!" He bit his lip.

*

Still he stared challengingly at the gleaming mechanism on the peak. An idea slowly took form in his mind; an exclamation abruptly escaped him. Narrowly he eyed the trussed girders of the silver towers which supported the great ring, muttering to himself.

"Yes, I can do it! If I don't get caught! I can climb it, well enough. The needle looks a bit frail. I should be able to smash it! I'd like to see Helen again, though."

21

THE DOOM FROM PLANET 4

He gathered the sheet around him, and began picking a cautious way up the canyon, staying always in the cover of boulders or brush. A few times he disturbed a rock, or snapped a twig beneath his foot. Then he waited out of sight for long minutes, though he had no reason to believe that the metal monsters were on the alert for him.

"I've got to do it! The world depends on it!" he kept saying again and again in his mind.

The quick darkness of the tropics had fallen almost before he started. But he welcomed the night, for, if it made his own silent progress more difficult, it reduced the hazard that he would be discovered.

Gauging the time by the slow wheeling of the diamond-like stars across the velvet sky, he thought that two hours had passed when he reached the head of the canyon. He stood up cautiously to survey the little plateau at the summit of the hill.

It was several acres in extent, quite level, and almost clear of vegetation. At the farther side was a pile of wreckage, which, he supposed, had been the quarters of Dr. Hunter's party, before they had been destroyed.

Many huge machines stood about the plateau, vast, dark masses looming in the starlight. Mostly they were either not running or very silent in operation; but a very deep, vibrant humming sound came from one near him. Smaller shapes were moving about them, with long easy leaps. These, he knew, were the mechanical monsters, though it was too dark to distinguish them.

*

But by far the most prominent object upon the plateau was the enormous gleaming thing that Helen had said was the station over which came the signals from the Master Intelligence on Mars. One of its three towers sprang up not far from where he stood. The huge, refulgent ring, swathed in its mist of purple fire, was a full hundred feet above him; and the slender needle, pulsing with white flame, swinging within and below the colossal ring, was itself a hundred feet in length.

The white needle, for all its length, seemed hardly thicker than a man's finger. It was mounted at the top of a curiously complex and delicate-looking device that spread broadly out between the three towers, below the center of the huge purple ring.

Dan looked at it and decided that his plan had at least a chance of success—though he had no hope that it would not be fatal to him.

Quickly and silently he ran to the base of the mighty silver towers nearest him and began to climb the side toward the ravine, where the maze of girders would hide him, at least partially, from any watchers back on the plateau. The starlight and the faint weird radiance of the purple ring above sufficed to guide him.

The cross-braces on the girder he had chosen were spaced closely enough to serve as the rungs of a ladder. Dan climbed easily, pausing twice for breath, and to look down at the dark plateau. The vast, humming machines loomed up strangely in the pale purple light that fell from the gleaming ring.

Once he looked across toward the other side of the island. The surface there was more level. He glimpsed tiny moving lights, and huge stationary masses, apparently as large as ocean liners. He had an impression of a vast amount of mechanical activity, proceeding in the darkness very rapidly, and in a silent and orderly fashion.

"The expeditionary force of the Master Intelligence of Mars," he thought, "preparing to set out against humanity! And what I can do is the only chance to stop it!"

*

He climbed again with renewed energy. A few yards more brought him to the colossal metal ring. Resting upon the three towers, it was a circular band of shining metal a foot thick and as wide as a road. The intense purple glow extended several feet from its surface.

Dan touched it tentatively. He felt a tingling electric shock. And he thought he could feel a radiation coming from it, giving him a curious sensation of cold. As he reached his hands up and grasped the upper edge of the great ring, he felt what seemed a physical current of cold.

THE DOOM FROM PLANET 4

Controlling his tendency to shiver, he climbed upon the last brace, and, lifting his weight with his hands, threw himself face down upon the flat upper surface of the vast ring. He lay bathed in cold purple fire. He tingled with the chill of it. A frozen current seemed to penetrate his body. Involuntarily he trembled, lost his grip and dangled precariously from the rim.

Only a frantic scrambling restored his hold. Then, fighting the sensation of freezing cold that came from the mist of purple flame, he drew himself forward and got to his feet upon the broad surface of the metal ring. On both sides it curved away like a circular track. Red-violet fire shimmered about it, bathing him to the waist in a chilling torrent.

Through coruscating frozen flame he waded to the inner rim of the colossal ring. Below him hung the needle, a mere straight line of white fire, a hundred feet in length. Eye-dazzling radiance scintillated along it, waxing and waning with a curious throbbing rhythm. The needle vibrated a little, but it pointed directly at the red point of Mars, now almost directly overhead.

Repressing a shudder, Dan looked down at the complex and delicate apparatus upon which the slender needle was mounted. It was a light frame of white metal bars, with spidery coils and huge glowing tubes and flimsy spinning disks mounted in it. The gleaming needle was mounted much like a telescope at the top of the device, fully fifty feet below him.

"Looks flimsy enough," Dan muttered. "I'll go through it like a sixteen-inch shell! Who would have thought I'd end this way!"

*

He stepped back for a moment, and stood on the polished metal, hidden to the waist in cold purple flame. Lest it impede his movements, he tore the sheet from him and threw it aside. He let his eyes sweep for a last time over the familiar constellations blazing so splendidly in the black sky above. He had a pang of heartache, as if the stars were old friends. His glance roved fondly over the dark, indistinct masses of the island, and across the black plain of the sea.

"Well, no good in waiting," he muttered again. "Sorry I can't see Helen. Hope she gets off all right."

He backed to the outer rim and drew a deep breath, like one about to dive. Then, with set face, he sprinted forward. As he did so a blinding flash of green light flickered up before him. He ducked his head and leapt from the inner edge of the vast glowing ring.

For long seconds, it seemed, he was plunging down through space, feet first. Air rushed screaming about his ears. But his mind was quite calm, and registered an astonishingly large series of impressions.

He saw the delicate, gleaming machine rushing up to meet him, the shimmering white needle swung on its top.

He took in the silent, dark plateau, with the masses of the great machines rising like ominous shadows here and there, and the mechanical monsters leaping busily about it, almost invisible in the dim, ghostly radiance that fell from the purple ring.

He saw a vivid flame of green reach up past him from somewhere below. He knew, without emotion or alarm, that he had been discovered, and that it was too late for his discoverers to stop him.

He found time, even, for a fleeting thought of death. His mind framed the question, "What will I be in a moment from now?"

Then he had struck the great white needle, and was crashing into the delicate apparatus below it. Waves of pain beat upon his mind like flashes of blinding light. But his last mental image, as he passed into oblivion, was a picture of Helen's face. Oddly, it was not her face as he had last seen it, but a reproduction of the old newspaper half-tone, curiously retouched with life and color.

*

There is little more to tell. It was some weeks later when Dan came back out of a world of delirium and dreams, to find himself lying on his back in a tent, very much bandaged. He was alone at the moment, and at first could not recall that tremendous last day of his conscious life.

Then he heard a thrillingly familiar feminine voice calling "Kitty, kitty, kitty." He tried to move, a dull pain throbbed in his breast, and a groan escaped him. In a moment Helen appeared; the gray kitten was forgotten. She looked very anxious and solicitous—and also, Dan thought, very beautiful.

"No, no!" she cried. "You are going to be all right! Dad made me learn a little elementary medicine before we came here, and I know. But you mustn't speak! Not for days yet! I'll have to guess what you want. And you can wink when I guess the right thing.

"Gee, but I'm glad you've come to! You'll be as well as ever, pretty soon. The kitten was lots of comfort. Still—"

Dan attempted to move. She leaned over him, shifted his weight and smoothed the sheet with strong, capable hinds. "You want to know about what happened to the machine monsters?"

He winked.

"Well, you remember when they found us, and shot the green ray at us. They left you there—I thought you were dead—and carried me up here on the hill. Perhaps they wanted me for a laboratory subject to test the green ray on, or something of the kind. Anyhow, they carried me into a big shed filled with strange machines.

"They kept me there until that night. Then, all of a sudden, they all—stopped! They froze! They were dead!

"The tentacles of the one that was holding me were set about me. But I worked free, and got out of the shed. It took all night. And when I came out, just at sunrise, I saw that the purple fire was gone from the great ring. The needle was knocked down, and the apparatus smashed.

"I found you there in the wreckage. You made a human bullet of yourself to smash it! The greatest thing a man ever did!"

*

Though normally rather modest, Dan felt a glow of pride at the honest admiration ringing in her clear voice, and shining from her warm brown eyes.

"So I gathered up what was left of you," she went on, "and tried to put you back together again. A good many bones were broken, and you had more cuts and bruises than I could mention; but the apparatus had broken the force of the fall, and you were still alive. You are remarkably well put together, I should say; and unusually lucky, as well!

"And, well, the machines and apparatus are scattered about all over the island. Every one of them stopped the instant you smashed the connection with the directing intelligence on Mars. There'll be quite a stir in the scientific world, I imagine, in about three weeks, when the yacht comes and carries us back with a lot of plans and specimens. We must send about a thousand engineers back here to study what we leave behind us.

"And do you want anything else?" She bent over and watched his bandaged face. Looking up into her bright eyes, thrilling to the cool, comforting pressure of her hand on his forehead, Dan reflected. Then he winked.

"Something you want me to do?"

He winked.

"When? Right now?"

No response.

"After the yacht comes."

He winked.

"What is it?" She looked him in the eye, blushed a little, and laughed.

"You mean—"

Dan winked.

www.ingramcontent.com/pod-product-compliance
Lightning Source LLC
Chambersburg PA
CBHW050910120626
46554CB00003B/1115